MW01180786

Syracuse, N.Y. 13219

3/01 Gift/Millbrook Press 16.43

Get in the Game! With Robin Roberts

SPORTS

FOR

LIFE

HOW ATHLETES HAVE MORE FUN

The Millbrook Press
Brookfield, Connecticut

The author and publisher wish to thank
Bill Gutman for his research and writing
contributions to this series.

Published by The Millbrook Press, Inc.
2 Old New Milford Road
Brookfield, Connecticut 06804
www.millbrookpress.com

Cover photograph courtesy of Steve Fenn/ABC
Photographs courtesy of Allsport: pp. 1 (© Jed
Jacobsohn), 31 (© Todd Warshaw), 41 (© Jed
Jacobsohn); Patrick Flynn: p. 4; Corbis: pp. 6 (©
Philip James Corwin), 24 (© Robert Maass), 33 (©
Wally McNamee); © Robert Beck/Icon SMI: pp.
10, 15, 20, 27, 37, 44 (left); Photo Edit: pp. 11 (©
Rudi Von Briel), 13 (© Frank Siteman), 16 (©
Michael Newman), 25 (© Myrleen Ferguson-Cate),
38 (© Gary A. Conner), 44 (right © Davis Barber);
Archive Photos: p. 19 (© Reuters/Dan LeClair);
Sports Illustrated: p. 32 (© Bob Donnan); © John
McDonough/Icon SMI: p. 34

Library of Congress Cataloging-in-Publication Data
Roberts, Robin, 1960–
Sports for life: how athletes have more fun
p. cm— (Get in the game! with Robin Roberts)
Includes index.
Summary: Explains how lifelong participation in
sports promotes health, confidence, and life
skills, and how girls can get the most out of vari-
ous levels of competition.
ISBN 0-7613-1407-5 (lib. bdg.)
ISBN 0-7613-1027-4 (pbk.)
1. Sports for children—United States—Juvenile lit-
erature. 2. Sports for children—United States—
Psychological aspects—Juvenile literature.
[1. Sports.] I. Title.
GV709.2 R53 2000 796'.083—dc21 00-024920

Copyright © 2000 by Affinity Communications
All rights reserved
Printed in the United States of America
5 4 3 2 1 (pbk.)
5 4 3 2 1 (lib. bdg.)

CONTENTS

Introduction

Sports have always been a big part of my life. From playing sandlot football with the other kids in my neighborhood in Biloxi, Mississippi, to playing tennis in high school and basketball in college, to working in sports broadcasting at ESPN, I can't imagine my life without sports. It used to be that girls who played sports were labeled "tomboys." These days, however, women and sports go hand-in-hand in so many ways.

Sports can increase a girl's confidence and help her to feel good about herself, and can help her succeed in nearly every aspect of life including school, a career, and relationships with friends and family.

With **Get in the Game!** my goal is to share my love and knowledge of the world of sports, and to show just how important sports can be. What you can learn on the field, court, rink, and arena are ways to solve problems, communicate with others, and become a leader. No matter what your skill level, if you learn all that sports can teach you, how can you *not* succeed at life in general? And the best part is that, like I have, you'll have fun at the same time!

—Robin Roberts

Although many girls
begin playing sports at a young age, it's never too late to start on the road to being a lifelong athlete.

Sports for Life

We live in a sports-oriented society. Millions of young girls begin playing soccer, softball, basketball, tennis, and other sports every year. Many will continue with sports and an active lifestyle right through high school. Then the best of the best will go on to play at the college level. Finally a select few who have the talent and the drive can actually wind up playing for pay as professional athletes or for worldwide acclaim as Olympians or in the World Cup.

Sports serves a definite purpose in the lives of girls and women. Playing sports promotes good health and self-confidence and teaches qualities such as teamwork and the ability to deal with adverse situations. However, playing various sports for pure enjoyment and exercise isn't always as simple as it sounds. There can be many roadblocks for young athletes, and different kinds of pressures. Some of these can actually be harmful and turn a girl away from sports.

The trick is to play, have fun, make new friends, learn skills, and try hard. With this book, you can learn the benefits of lifelong participation in sports, whether or not you eventually become a star in the WNBA or a pro golfer winning big prizes. You don't have to be a professional athlete to make sports work for you. The things you learn, the character you build, and the skills you acquire through sports will help you in anything you do.

Starting Young

Attitudes toward girls playing sports, as well as playing at an early age, are changing all the time. How many times have you heard boys tease each other by saying, "You throw like a girl"? According to Dr. Mimi Murray, a professor of sports psychology at Springfield College in Springfield, Massachusetts, there is a good reason for the difference. "Girls weren't learning the motor patterns needed for many sports skills, such as throwing a ball," Dr. Murray explains. In other words, girls weren't traditionally taught the correct way to throw a ball.

Like many others involved with athletes and athletics, Dr. Murray feels that it's very important for girls to begin with sports early. "If a girl is not active or involved with sports by age 12, chances are she will never start," Dr. Murray says. "By that age, she might feel she looks foolish if she tries to do something she has never done before."

Girls can begin developing their motor skills and coordination at an early age. There was a time when a girl who showed an early love for sports was called a "tomboy." The name was insulting and probably caused some girls to stop playing. Fortunately, many of those stereotypes have disappeared. Today, young girls who love sports are seen simply as athletes. Because the world of women's sports has grown so much, playing sports is looked upon as just another activity for a girl.

Girls who play sports at an early age begin to absorb the benefits almost immediately. Playing and being able to do something well can make you feel good right away. Just to hear people say, "You're good," gives you a good feeling. To have boys pick you to play on their team also gives you a great deal of satisfaction. That's right—there's no reason that boys and girls shouldn't play together when they are young

It's important for young female athletes to learn basic skills, such as the proper way to throw a ball, that were once taught mainly to boys.

and just beginning to become involved with sports. They really can learn from each other.

"Young girls who play sports immediately take on a responsible attitude," explains Gretchen Seeley. Seeley coaches girls' basketball at a private high school in California and also runs an after-school basketball program, "Shoot for the Stars," for fourth- to eighth-grade girls in the East Palo Alto, California, community. "They learn to interact with their peers, solve their problems together, and get along. In other words, sports gives them an early lesson in making their environment work and it carries over to other things later in life."

The positive reasons to become involved with sports start early. And if you continue with sports, they only get better!

Girls and boys can learn a lot from each other when they play sports together. Anyone can benefit from playing with many different types of athletes.

The Importance of Good Coaching

By playing sports at an early age, you get in good physical shape and begin to find self-confidence and self-esteem. At the same time, you can have a great deal of fun. But you must also be watchful about what happens next. If you begin playing with a team, some things can change.

A good coach can help your development as a young athlete and give you the desire to continue to the next level. If a coach does his or her job correctly, you will come away with a sense of confidence and accomplishment. Mastering sports skills can make anyone feel good, and the self-confidence that comes with it can carry over to other areas of your life, such as school.

A good coach of young athletes always praises success and minimizes his or her own reactions to failure. This kind of positive reinforcement can help you as a player feel sure of yourself. Young athletes should know from the beginning

Developing a good relationship

with your coach can make a big difference in your growth as an athlete. A good coach has much to teach you about both your sport and being an athlete in general.

that winning isn't the most important thing in life. If you have a bad game or make a bad play, it isn't the end of the world. A good coach understands this, and knows how to keep the fun in sports for his or her players.

Some coaches, however, tend to make winning and losing too impor-tant. Gretchen Seeley feels that every young athlete should get to play in every game. "No kid should have to sit on the bench the entire game," she says. "Letting everyone play should be the important thing. Winning and losing should not be a deciding factor."

Playing is fun, and not having pressure to win at a young age keeps it fun. Sometimes, however, youngsters get frustrated with sports early on. It might be because of the pressure to win, or because of coaches who yell and scream, and who sometimes even resort to personal insults. No young athlete should be placed in this situation. If you feel your coach is not treating you right, you should talk to your parents. If this happens, always be truthful and state the facts.

"You can't yell at kids and expect to get anything from them, especially the very young ones," Seeley says. "Yelling is a turn-off. Yet I'm seeing more yelling creeping into girls' programs. And, believe it or not, I am also seeing some cheating in sports programs. Coaches sometimes bring in older players who should be in the next age group. They do this because they want to win. Yet if winning were made mandatory, kids would be under too much pressure and would never learn how to lose well."

Dr. Murray is also concerned about these problems. One of the things she would like to see is girls and boys playing and working together in sports at a young age. She feels that both can learn from each other. But it's important that coaches remain fair.

"Coaches sometimes tend to favor the boys," Dr. Murray explains. "But girls need as much skill reinforcement as boys do. I've noticed that when men are coaching teams with both girls and boys, they tend to give girls general instruction while they give boys help with specific things. In other words, they some-

It's important for a coach to teach all skills to all athletes, whether girls or boys. This wrestling coach takes time with a female member of his team.

times coach the boys much more closely."

Dr. Murray also feels that coaches of teams with both boys and girls should make sure that everyone gets to play important positions. A coach should be teaching all the skills to all the players, and not focus on whether the team wins or loses the game.

It is important for a young athlete to have a strong support group around her. This can include friends with similar interests, supportive families, and a good coach who can teach new skills, be positive, not focus on winning or losing, refrain from yelling and humiliating young athletes, and—most of all—make sure that sports always remains fun.

As you progress and

grow with sports, the competition—as well as the
pressure on you as an athlete and on how you
work with your team—gets more intense.

Getting Better at Sports

When an athlete reaches the middle-school and high-school levels, the meaning of sports begins to change. The early years are the best time to experiment and try a lot of different sports just for the pure fun of it. But by the time you reach high school, you will probably begin to concentrate on your best sport or two, or even three for the top athletes. At that level, there will be more emphasis on winning, and the best players will get the most playing time.

For all young athletes, one of the keys to success is maintaining a balance in their lives. In other words, sports must be balanced with academics, and also with a social life. Athletes will find new pressures as they get older, especially when they move from middle school to high school. Therefore, you should always try to be your own watchdog. If you find yourself practicing your sport more, but your grades are going down, for example, then it's time to cut back on the practice time.

Always remember to balance your life. Allow yourself to still be a teenager and enjoy different things. Be a good student and a good friend. You can do all this and still be an outstanding athlete.

One thing you will sense as a high-school athlete is a change in the focus of team sports. Now, there is more emphasis on winning. There is a great deal of competition between high schools, and a lot of pride at stake when two high schools meet in athletic competition. By the same token, if you have been involved with sports since elementary school and love to play, you will also begin to think more about winning, as well as about how far you can go as an athlete. Some players like the feeling of being one of the best and are very goal-oriented.

Many are also thinking about college and the possibility of earning a scholarship through their athletic ability.

Obviously, there can be both joys and pitfalls for you at this level. Gretchen Seeley sounds a warning when she says, "I see a kind of cockiness begin to creep into some good athletes at the high-school level. Along with that sometimes comes a huge loss of joy in playing the sport. It's kind of sad to see. On the other hand, I have also noticed at the high-school level that the kids who don't play regularly, those on the bench, seem to still have that childlike sense of wonder, that pure joy of being part of a team and playing a sport."

There is no reason why all athletes cannot retain this sense of joy. After all, you and your teammates are working together to become a

winning team. You can forge a cama-
raderie that will last forever from
working for a common goal. Sports
is also a form of entertainment. You
and your teammates can bring that
same sense of joy to your family,
friends, classmates, and all those
who come to watch the team play. A
team playing well, working together,
and enjoying the competition is a
joy to watch.

But there is also no getting away
from the fact that we live in a very
competitive world, with a great pre-
mium placed on winning. The word
winner is equated with success; a
loser is looked upon as a failure. It
shouldn't be that way. No one can
win all the time and no one is mis-
take-free, not even the best of them.
Athletes like Mia Hamm, Cynthia
Cooper, Venus Williams, and Tara
Lipinski have all made mistakes. Yet
all have risen to the top because

they enjoy their sports and can
accept the fact that they aren't perfect. The great Michael Jordan,
arguably the best basketball player
ever, is a prime example of playing
for the right reasons. Even with all
his success, his fierce competitiveness, and his
will to win,

**Tennis star Venus
Williams is at
the top of her
game, yet even
she doesn't
win every time.
The best athletes
accept that
mistakes and
failure go hand
in hand with
victory.**

A good coach will accept individual mistakes as part of the game, and can accept losses, too, if the team gives its all each time it plays.

basketball was, above all, always fun. He loved his sport and expressed joy in simply being able to play and compete.

Trying to retain your joy in playing and learning to accept losing are lessons you will have to learn as a young athlete. Everyone will have the experience of losing to a better team or player. Losing can make some athletes work harder to improve their skills. At the same time, there are some young athletes who begin to do anything to win, even if good sportsmanship isn't part of it. This can happen when an athlete is made to feel that winning is the only acceptable outcome.

It isn't. If you always play your best and try your hardest to win, no one can ask anything more. As Gretchen Seeley says, "If you have a weak basketball team, for example, you can't realistically expect to have a 20-win season." Your coach should realize this as well, because if a coach puts unrealistic pressure to win on a team and its players, that can only hurt everyone. If the coach sees that you and your teammates are giving 100 percent, have stayed in great physical condition, and never give up, then he or she has to accept the results. You and your teammates are winners, no matter what the score.

It can certainly be upsetting if you, as an individual, make a mistake. But you shouldn't jump all over teammates for a mistake, even if it results in the loss of the game. Remember, no one makes a mistake intentionally, and no one wants to make a mistake that costs her team the game. You and your team will be better served if you tell your teammate to forget about the mistake, that you should all concentrate on winning the next game. That is posi-

tive reinforcement, something every player and each coach should practice. A player who wants to be the best she can be has to keep her confidence at a high level. An unthinking teammate or coach can often help destroy that confidence.

Everyone has to realize that bad plays happen to even the best players. You may have dropped the ball that allowed the winning run to score in a 2–1 loss. But if your team scored just one run, then no one really hit well, either. Look at it that way. No athlete should have to live with a "what if."

There are going to be some other potential roadblocks as a young athlete progresses. Dr. Murray explains that a difficult time can occur when a girl goes through her adolescent years. Her body is changing and, as a result, she may feel more self-conscious and lose some of her confidence. If you feel this is happening to you, speak to your coach, your parents, or a teacher about it. You've got to understand that this, too, will pass. If you are actively involved in sports, you will soon be able to cope with the changes, you will grow stronger, and in most cases your performance will soon begin to improve.

During this same period there are some athletes who begin taking sports too seriously. This is where maintaining a balance once again becomes important. For example, are you talking about sports and nothing else? Are your grades beginning to go downward? Have you stopped seeing some of your old friends who don't play sports? Are you training so much that you are constantly tired, with no time for much else? These are all signs that you might be making sports too big a part of your life. Being single-minded like this will not help you as

an athlete and will not make your high-school years happy ones. Work hard and play hard, but still enjoy school, family, and friends. Make this a happy and productive time of your life.

Sports can enhance your overall satisfaction with life. Whether you plan to play in college or not, enjoy participating in high-school sports to the fullest. There is nothing wrong with being competitive and wanting to win. Those qualities will help you not only in sports but in other areas of your life as well. However, if you live and die by each game, each missed shot, each strikeout, or each error, then you are doing yourself a grave disservice. This isn't what sports is all about. Sports should reinforce positive values, help you to be physically fit and healthy, and teach you to work with others as part of a team striving for the same goals.

What If You're Not Good Enough?

Many millions of young girls and boys begin playing sports each year. Soon, the majority of them are playing in an organized league. It could be at their school, in their town, in a church YWCA, or YMCA league, or in an after-school street program. Sports is an extremely well-organized industry in the United States, with many programs designed to teach youngsters and keep them interested.

However, as young players become older, many start dropping out of sports for a number of reasons. Some may simply not enjoy sports enough; others may not be good enough to keep up with their peers. Some quit because of a bad coach, peer pressure, or even problems at home. Others have to go to work to earn extra money as soon as they're old enough. Finally, there are some who love to play and compete, and who dream about playing at the next level, but suddenly realize that they aren't good enough to reach that level.

You may have been "number one" at your sport as a youngster, but as you grow you'll notice that the competition is stiffer. Finding that you don't have what it takes to compete at a higher level, though, doesn't have to mean giving up sports altogether.

As you become older, you will be playing against better competitors. You will be playing against teams from other towns or other schools. If you happen to be the best on your team or at your school, you might begin to realize that there are better players elsewhere. That can be a difficult thing to accept at first. It makes some players work harder, but others simply give up. Those who continue on to high-school athletics may suddenly find that they are no longer starters, but substitutes. And those who were looking forward to playing in college might discover that they are just not good enough to play at that level. What then? Is their sporting life over? It certainly doesn't have to be.

If this happens to you, the first thing you must realize is that not being good enough is okay. Every athlete can't be a star in high school, and every high-school star cannot go on to play at the college level. If you are capable of being your own best and worst critic, you may realize your limitations without having to be told. Otherwise, however, you need a solid core group of supporters—friends, coaches, or family members who will be real with you.

There may be some disappointment at first. In fact, many athletes will wonder why they bothered to work so hard and train for so long. They feel that not being good enough is a sign of failure. It isn't. The things you learned from sports—discipline, competitiveness, a desire to be the best you can be, a solid work ethic—will stay with you always. In this sense, the good far outweighs the bad.

It's okay to be disappointed if someday you aren't "good enough." Even if you show your disappointment, you are also showing that you care, that you are passionate, and that you are human. It is important to think back and remember those moments when you did reach your goal in sports, when you did achieve something you set out to do. But it's still all right to feel hurt. In time, you will pick yourself up and continue reaping the benefits of an athletic lifestyle.

If you find yourself not stacking up to the competition in your favorite sport, you can view it as an opportunity to explore a variety of other sports and activities.

The one thing you shouldn't do is quit sports completely. If you do that, you are also giving up a healthy, active lifestyle. If you loved sports once, that love should remain, even if you aren't competing at the level you once wanted to.

"Being physically active is healthy. It's as simple as that," Dr. Murray explains. "There are fewer teen suicides, unwanted pregnancies, and school dropouts among girls who are involved in some form of sports. The statistics tell us that girls involved with sports are 92 percent less likely to become involved with drugs, 80 percent less likely to have that unwanted pregnancy, and three times more likely to graduate high school. That doesn't mean you have to play on the varsity team. These statistics describe girls who are physically active and engage in sports on any level.

"In high school," Dr. Murray adds, "the athletes tend to be among the top achievers, academically as well as in sports, and aspire to go to college more than those who don't participate and aren't physically active."

Just because you didn't make your high-school or college team, there are still other ways to compete. It may not be on the level you had hoped for, but it is still sports and it still means having an active lifestyle and competing against players on your level. It can be in a town league, an intramural program in high school or college, or just pick-up games with your friends. You can also learn new sports, perhaps individual activities such as tennis, running, martial arts, skiing, snowboarding, or mountain and rock climbing. These are activities that you can pursue for years to come.

One of the greatest things about sports is that there are so many activities to choose from. What's more, there are many opportunities and ways to participate at every level.

At the same time, you can channel your energy to the classroom and other productive ventures.

The struggle to improve and reach the next level in sports was probably filled with pressure and anxiety. If you play in intramural and other less structured leagues, and play for the competition and exercise, chances are you will rediscover the pure joy of sports, the kind of feeling you had when you began playing in the first place.

Sports and an athletic lifestyle do not exclude anyone. Handicapped people have done some incredible things. Those confined to wheelchairs play basketball and participate in marathon races. People who are missing a leg have skied down steep mountains and have gone hang gliding. There is no limit to what you can do in sports. You don't have to be playing for the Houston Comets or the United States National Soccer Team to get the most from your body and from competition. Everyone cannot be an elite athlete. Accept your ability and talent for what it is, and continue on from there with enthusiasm and zeal.

What If You Are Good Enough?

When a young athlete realizes she isn't quite good enough to play at the next level, she has to make adjustments. She must learn to look at the positives, pursue other ventures such as her education, and, it is to be hoped, continue to live a healthy, athletic lifestyle. But athletes who *are* good enough, who have the opportunity to play their sports at the college level and perhaps beyond, must also make adjustments. They are about to experience something special—playing their sports at a high level with other top athletes. It is something that may last only a few short years. Any girl talented enough to make it to this level should enjoy every minute of it.

Star athletes are sometimes looked upon as heroes and, as such, often get special treatment. For that reason, it is important to keep your life in order and your priorities straight. There is nothing inherently wrong with being very good at something, whether it's sports or some other activity. No matter what it is, however, it cannot become an obsession. While a top athlete may have to make some sacrifices (she may have to skip a party now and then, go home early to get that extra few hours of sleep, and practice when her friends are doing something else), she can't forget the other things that are important—family, friends, and her studies. A top athlete is still in school and must get good grades, especially if she wants to go to college.

A perfect example of someone who was able to keep this kind of balance and perspective is Cynthia Cooper, who was the Most Valuable Player in the WNBA in the league's first two years. Cooper also led her team, the Houston Comets, to three straight WNBA championships. But there was a time when it seemed she would never have that kind of opportunity. Cynthia's mother, Mary Cobbs, raised eight children in a ghetto area of Los Angeles, California. The neighborhood was riddled with crime. Gangs and drugs seemed to be everywhere. It would have been very easy for a youngster to go in the wrong direction. But this was something Cynthia Cooper was able to see early in life.

"When I was a kid, I was very shy," she says. "And I had a lot of negative influences around me. I didn't know what I wanted to do with my life then, but I definitely knew what I didn't want to do."

What Cynthia didn't want to do was run with the gangs. Instead, she turned to sports, first playing softball, then running track. Soon, she was a track star in the Los Angeles school system. By the time she was in her teen years she was developing the kind of character that would bring her eventual success. She was also beginning to play basketball. Much of the credit for her desire to excel and go on to the next level goes to her mother. Cynthia Cooper has always said that her mother is her hero.

"I couldn't run track or play basketball unless my grades were together," Cooper has said. "Academics were always very important. I've also always had this fire that burns inside of me that says I can do it, that I can accomplish anything I've set my mind to. I got that from my mother, as well, and I never let anyone put out that fire."

Years later, when Cooper was a star at the University of Southern California, she learned that one of her younger brothers had been stabbed to death in a gang fight. "Nothing seemed worth it any more," she said, speaking of her reaction to the tragedy. Then the support group around her— her family, coaches, and friends— made her realize that basketball and college meant too much to her to give them up. She persevered and finally triumphed.

As a top high-school athlete, you may have a chance to be offered a college scholarship. That means your entire four-year education will be paid for as you continue your sports career. Scholarships are great opportunities for athletes to attend colleges they might otherwise not be able to afford. To find the best student athletes, college scouts and recruiters visit high schools to talk with prospects and watch them play. For some high-school stars, knowing they are being recruited can mean some added pressure to perform well. Surprisingly, some of that pressure might come from home.

WNBA superstar Cynthia Cooper
one of the elite few who has made it to the top of her sport. Not only
is she a superb athlete, her perseverance and drive helped her to
overcome many obstacles to pursue her dream.

Mia Hamm was a successful college athlete at the University of North Carolina who also rose to the top of her game with the 1999 United States World Cup Soccer championship team.

"Sometimes parents put pressure on their child to get a scholarship," says Dr. Murray. "There are not that many scholarship openings and many hopeful high-school athletes will not receive one. It's up to the parents to let their daughter know that they will love her no matter what happens, and that not getting a scholarship has nothing to do with her value as a person. In other words, not getting a scholarship should not be looked upon as a sign of failure."

Gretchen Seeley has noticed the same kind of pressure coming from high-school girls themselves. "Women's sports has become so big now that there is almost an illusion that everyone can do it," Seeley says. "Too many girls are now thinking about being stars and not thinking that they are going to get an education as well."

Some athletes may think that aiming for a scholarship means they have to concentrate strictly on sports. They forget the importance of getting an education and a college degree that can lead to a productive career in future years. While it's great to be able to play on a top-flight college team, or to compete in individual sports on the collegiate level, after four years it's over. There are very few professional opportunities for women athletes, especially when you think about the numbers of women competing at the college level. An education and a diploma give you something that can work for you for the rest of your life.

What are the considerations for a college sports scholarship? The academic requirements may vary somewhat from school to school, but there are certain qualities that all coaches and recruiters look for in high-school athletes. Amy Tucker, the associate head basketball coach at Stanford University, recruits high-school athletes as part of her job. She looks for both general and specific things when trying to fill the scholarship slots at Stanford.

A college-level athlete should balance her participation in sports with her studies. In most cases, she will need her college degree to get a good job after college and her athletic "career" have ended.

Stanford University
has the right idea when it comes to recruiting athletes: They look at academic achievement as well as athletic achievement. Pictured here is Jamila Wideman, now a star with the WNBA Portland Fire.

"Stanford has always had very high academic standards," she says. "So our first requirement for a scholarship is that the athlete must also be in the top 10 percent of her high-school class. Other schools do not have these strict academic standards and can sign kids making the minimum passing grades as set down by the National Collegiate Athletic Association (NCAA)."

As a coach, scout, and recruiter, Tucker looks for little extras that are not always easy to see in prospective student athletes and also keeps an eye out for some not-so-great characteristics.

"For starters, we want someone who has a great work ethic, a great attitude, and who is dedicated to improving her skills. You can usually see a positive attitude in the way an athlete relates to her coach and teammates. If you see a high school kid yelling at her teammates or coach, that's a bad sign. Even if the player is a star and a perfectionist, we don't want someone who is going to argue with the coach and be constantly berating her teammates."

While she says that recruiting isn't a science and that there are always mistakes, certain things are a no-no right from the start.

"A bad work ethic won't improve," Coach Tucker explains. "We always try to handpick our scholarship players. They are going to have everything paid for at a school that also has a great academic program. So we want players who will stick around all four years."

There are a number of other ways to receive aid to attend college. Some girls who also happen to be fine athletes can receive academic scholarships for their out-standing work in the classroom. Such girls might even decide to attend a smaller college that doesn't give athletic scholarships, but where they can still have the joy and experience of participating in sports at the college level while receiving their higher educations. There are also various types of grants and aid available, as well as the possibility of student loans. High schools all have special counselors to help students find different ways to attend college. If you are a good athlete, but not quite good enough for a scholarship, don't give up. There are still ways to attend college and continue with sports at the same time.

For the special group good enough to get that full athletic scholarship, your hard work has paid off. It's a great feeling to know you've done it.

Sports at the College Level

As a high-school athlete, you worked to be the best you could be, kept your grades up, and also maintained a balance in your life. Once you get to college, however, you will find that things are very different than they were in high school. You will have to work even harder to keep up with your studies and, at the same time, you will find that your sport is more demanding and more competitive than it ever was before. Because of this, you will quickly discover that keeping your life balanced is more important than ever.

"Freshman players must almost always make an adjustment," Amy Tucker says. "All scholarship players were stars on their high-school teams, but once they get to college they have to realize there can't be 15 stars on the totem pole. Some have to start at the bottom."

If you are used to being a "big fish in a little pond," you may now find yourself a "little fish in a big pond." You will have to show maturity in dealing with this kind of change. If you succeed, chances are that you will not only become a prominent contributor within the program, but will also have success later in life.

Another adjustment, according to Amy Tucker, is learning to deal with a whole new group of teammates. It's something a player must do at any level, but in a big-time collegiate program, it becomes an

Continuing as a college athlete presents new challenges that the best of the best will meet successfully: Competition is tougher, there may be more pressure to win, and athletes may find that they are no longer the best on their team.

extremely impor-
tant issue.

"No one can
like everyone
else," she
explains. "Chances
are a player will
have a teammate
or two that she just
doesn't like. Yet

Another challenge for a college athlete is keeping up with classes and assignments. Often she will have to make personal sacrifices to succeed both athletically and academically.

out on the court she has to get along with those teammates, complement them as players, and not allow her personal feelings to interfere with the success of the team."

The balancing of sports and studies is probably the most important challenge you will face. At this stage of your athletic career, you may be at the highest level you will attain. Very few women go on to play basketball in the WNBA, for example, and there aren't too many other professional opportunities available. Because of this, the chance to come away with a college degree and an outstanding education cannot be overlooked. That takes work. In addition, the time you must devote to your sport at the college level is far greater than it ever was in high school. "During the season, an athlete probably spends three to five hours a day practicing," Coach Tucker explains. "Then there are classes and studying. What has to go? Usually it's a social life, the fun. Athletes, as a rule, can't really go out weeknights, not if they want to stay up on their academics and keep themselves physically ready to practice and play. Yet they also cannot become obsessed with just their sport. That's where finding a balance comes in."

Just as a high-school star should not make getting a scholarship her only goal, topflight college athletes shouldn't count on continuing with a professional career. This has been an old story for years with men. College baseball, basketball, and football players want to go on to the major leagues, the National Basketball Association (NBA), or the National Football League (NFL). Yet only a few make it. If those who don't make it fail to have an alternate plan, they can find themselves back at square one. Many never even complete their college educations.

Some women are beginning to think the same way. With the WNBA firmly established, and pro leagues for women spreading to sports such as softball and volleyball, many women are now talking about pro careers. But as a college star, you should also be sure to study hard and earn your degree. That way, you will have many opportunities to pursue after graduation.

"Stanford currently has eight graduates playing in the WNBA, but that doesn't guarantee an incoming freshman that she will also make it," Coach Tucker says. "I simply tell them to enjoy playing here for four years. And when the realization that they can't play pro sets in, all the girls are grateful that they have a college degree from Stanford."

Coach Tucker echoes what so many other people say about sports, namely that playing on a team and interacting with your teammates have positive effects that sometimes cannot be measured.

"Playing sports at all levels develops character," she said. "Women develop confidence that carries over when they enter the real world and the work force. Those involved with sports also develop life skills—dealing with teammates, peers, and even people they may not like. They learn to handle adversity.

"There's nothing quite as satisfying as watching a girl start out as a somewhat immature, socially awkward freshman and then play ball for four years. When she graduates, she's usually become a confident senior, like a flower that bloomed slowly over four years. She's now a totally different person and ready for whatever happens next."

There are some other stops a woman can make between college and a sporting lifestyle. Top athletes can try out for the United States Olympic Team. Representing your country in the Olympics—competing in either team or individual sports—can be a wonderful, exhilarating experience. In fact, you can have a great experience and make new friends just by trying out.

There are still other opportunities. The best soccer players get to represent the United States in World Cup competition every four years, while the United States also sends athletes to other world events such as the Pan American Games. Track stars can compete all over the world in various professional meets, and there are also potentially lucrative professional opportunities for

Postcollege athletic opportunities besides professional sports include representing the United States in the Olympics, at the World Cup (pictured), and in other international competitions.

golfers, tennis players, and figure skaters. Sports as an entertainment vehicle continues to grow and expand, with women playing an increasingly prominent role.

Whether college athletics is a stepping-stone for future sporting opportunities, or becomes the final stage for your big-time athletic career, don't waste an exciting opportunity. Play hard, study hard, get your degree, and find a way to continue pursuing a healthy, athletic lifestyle.

The Sporting Life

Kids begin playing sports because it's fun. At first, playing is fun all the time. Later it's fun when you win, not so much fun when you lose. Then it's fun if you're part of the starting team, but not so much fun if you're riding the bench. Finally, it's fun when you win and earn a college scholarship, but not so much fun if you lose and find you're not good enough to play at the college level.

An athlete can find a dozen reasons to quit playing at various times of her life. It can be a bad coach early on, or not starting on your high-school team later. If you look hard enough, you can always find a reason or an excuse to stop. You should realize, however, that playing organized sports means something more than winning or losing. In fact, it even means more than learning to be a team player and building character. In addition to these things, it means building and then sticking with an active, healthy lifestyle, something that can last a lifetime. Anyone who begins playing sports as a youngster can continue participating for the rest of her life, even long after the typical sports "career" is over.

This phase of a sports-oriented and active life can begin in high school or college. Maybe you weren't good enough to make the varsity in high school, or you aren't quite up to earning that college scholarship. It isn't difficult to move from the varsity to playing at the intramural level. If you don't attend college, you can also continue your sports career by playing in a town league, or within a recreational program at a school, church, YMCA, or YWCA. In addition, there are many things you can do as an individual, such as running, weight training, or aerobics. Now you're free to try other sports that maybe you enjoyed once, but weren't quite good enough to play at the school level.

College students who cannot play varsity sports have even more opportunities to continue with a sports-oriented lifestyle.

"At Stanford [University] there are no junior varsity (JV) sports," Amy Tucker explains. "But there are a wealth of opportunities for women who want an active lifestyle. There is a complete intramural sports program as well as several club teams. For example, there is a club rugby team for women and even a coed Frisbee team. These club teams travel and do what other varsity teams would do. The players involved all have a great time.

"There are also classes in sports, such as golf, horseback riding, and dance, just to name a few. Most of our athletes and athleti-

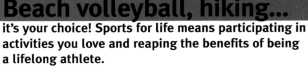

Beach volleyball, hiking...

it's your choice! Sports for life means participating in activities you love and reaping the benefits of being a lifelong athlete.

cally active women don't become couch potatoes. Many women are into being strong and fit. They stay with it, many of them for the rest of their lives."

There is very little doubt about the ultimate value of sports. The tough part is to approach sports and physical activity with the right atti-

tude, to surround yourself with good people, and not get too caught up in some of the traps that lie along the way. Kids begin playing for fun and later, as adults, they find they are once again playing for fun. It's what happens in between that is sometimes difficult.

Athletes are taught to win and to be the very best they can be. There is nothing wrong with that as long as it is kept in perspective. The majority of girls and women playing sports will never rise to the level of Cynthia Cooper, Mia Hamm, Jackie Joyner-Kersee, or Venus Williams. For elite athletes and professionals, sports is a business. Athletes, both female and male, have to be the best they can be, and they are paid to win. Unfortunately, many of today's professional athletes act as if they aren't having much fun.

For the average athlete and physically active person, sports should remain fun and become a way of life. If your sports career ends in high school or college, there can be other challenges. Instead of field hockey, take up rock climbing or snowboarding. To take the place of the excitement of sprinting, try distance running or even the challenge of the triathlon. If you no longer feel up to a challenge, but want to maintain fitness, there are many ways to achieve that.

The real value of sports isn't always a great shot you made to win a big game, or even that you might have been part of a championship team or that you may have risen to the top of your sport. Rather, it is the life skills that sports can teach you—self-confidence, discipline, a sense of achievement, and control over your health and your body. The things you learn and do to make yourself a healthy athlete will also make you healthier for life. Regular exercise, a good diet, the proper rest, and the ability to balance all the parts of your life will make you a winner. These are things learned by being a lifelong athlete with an active lifestyle.

It sure beats being a couch potato!

Get in the Game!

There are lots of exciting resources for lifelong female athletes. Here are a few books and Web sites, plus a great on-line magazine, to get you started on your search.

Girl Power on the Playing Field by Andy Steiner (Minneapolis: Lerner, 1999).
Girl to Girl: On Sports by Anne Driscoll (New York: Element, 2000).
Good Sports: Winning. Losing. And Everything in Between by Therese Kauchak (Middleton, WI: American Girl Library, 1999).
Play Like a Girl: A Celebration of Women in Sports edited by Sue Macy and Jane Gottesman (New York: Henry Holt, 1999).
Winning Every Day: Gold Medal Advice for a Happy, Healthy Life! by Shannon Miller and Nancy Ann Richardson (New York: Bantam, 1998).

members.aol.com/msdaizy/sports/locker.html
   The Locker Room explores sports for younger kids.
www.melpomene.org
   The Melpomene Institute Web site explores the link between physical activity and health for women.
www.feminist.org/sports/sports.html
   This site looks at various aspects of women in sports, including the Olympics, and has links to additional Internet resources.
www.womenssportsfoundation.org
   A good, basic site for all you want to know about women in sports.
www.gogirlmag.com
   Go, Girl! is a fun, on-line sports magazine.

Index